as it HAPPENED

THE VIRAL TALES

PRASANNA CHOUDHARY

INDIA • SINGAPORE • MALAYSIA

ISBN 979-8-89133-384-0

This book is dedicated to all people, from all walks of life, who have served humanity during the toughest time.

Contents

Preface

Life is beautiful. God gives life to a soul. It comes into the world and the journey begins. Inside a mother's womb, its world appears to be the best, undisturbed by what is happening outside. Having come into the world, it has to follow the protocol of breathing from day one. Mother Earth becomes a human being's only Karma battleground because humans, as we know, do not exist on any other planet in the solar system.

The world is grappling with a life-threatening virus that has shaken it up. During this time, 'as It Happened' is the journey of many souls – tiny happy creatures who are still in their mothers' wombs, young ones who are ready to chase their dreams as well as old souls who have seen the various shades of life.

I am very thankful to every person who has contributed to this book, directly or indirectly.

Special thanks to a beautiful tiny soul, for being a source of inspiration for this book.

Place: Somewhere in India

Time: 2 AM

Date: 23rd March 2020

The Journey Begins...

Part I

A Walk of a Thousand Miles

A few days back – 5th March 2020

5.45 AM. The alarm rings.

A month ago, I began attending yoga classes and now I wake up early to prepare myself for the class. I have come to enjoy this routine as it infuses energy into my entire day. The intense yet soothing practice of yoga, which helps connect my body, mind and breath, is the perfect workout for an average-built non-athletic person like me. The fresh air around me instils a sense of meditation, while the melodies of the chirping birds introduce new rhythms into my daily life.

At around 6 AM, I got a call from an unknown number.

I declined the call, which was an automated wake-up reminder from my yoga centre. In this modern age, even our training authorities provide wake-up calls to motivate their Yogic students to attend the class. If one is committed, they can jump right out of bed and head to an early morning class. I appreciate the dedication of the exceptional trainers at the yoga centre as they ensure I do not miss out on any of the workout or yoga sessions. Exercising every day for an hour or attending a yoga session leaves one feeling rejuvenated all day long.

It is Springtime – a duration between winter and summer when plants start to grow, flowers bloom and new leaves start to sprout. During this time, the ice on the mountaintop starts melting and flows gently through the rocky mountain trails. Birds, with their uplifting spirit, break the silence through their sweet sounds as they go hunting for new shelters. Every bit of nature turns into a refreshing green shade like an energizing spirit, ready to lift its charisma. And in Bengaluru, it blooms in a unique way.

I am fond of the spring season, which comes for a short duration after winter. It lifts the spirit when one gets to see new leaves on the trees, blossoming flowers and the uplifting mood of the surrounding climate. Being in the city of Bengaluru allows me to visit several entrancing places nearby. And why not? After all, Bengaluru is famous for many nature nests that are perfect for weekend getaways and vacations. Most of India's tourist destinations flourish during this season.

For many years, I, Prasad, have not been a morning person. However, this time, I had decided to make a change in the way my life was going. While changes are inevitable, those brought on by oneself can bring about positive vibes.

"Is the lunchbox ready?" my wife Gauri messaged me. She has been in her hometown since the last week of January. She is a soft-spoken person and has the voice of a good singer.

I responded, "Yes, I have prepared Sago." Sago is a small, white, round grain that is typically consumed during fasting. I have been preparing my own meals for the past few days. Even though I was tired of eating outside food, given the current situation in the world and India, I found it more comforting to cook both lunch and dinner. In the last few months, a virus has been rapidly spreading in several countries, including India. It started in China around December and had already reached the USA by January. Unfortunately, there is no vaccine available for this virus. Although there were no reported cases in Bengaluru, I had decided to take precautions, nonetheless. I was tired of eating in the office cafeteria and outside food or ordering from the various food apps most of the time, so I had planned to prepare my lunch as much as possible.

My office is quite near to home. I am usually able to skip the well-known humongous Bengaluru traffic by taking another short route to work, making it an easy daily commute.

I reached the office in 15 minutes. After parking the bike in the basement and passing through the office security, I walked into the lobby lift and pressed 11 on the right-hand side panel to reach my work floor. Our office lifts have an even-odd system. One side of the lift stops on even-numbered floors while the other side stops on the odd-numbered ones.

11.30 AM – Tea-break

"When are you going to your hometown, Prasad?" my friend and colleague asked while we sat in the cafeteria on our floor. We were gazing out at the high-rise buildings and the lake covered with green shells in the distance.

"I am going to my wife's hometown, not mine. I will leave tonight. The flight is at 5 in the morning," I responded with a child-like smile on my face as I sipped green tea.

"For how many days are you going?" he asked while sipping coffee.

"Only 3 days," I told him in a quick response.

After chatting for another half an hour, we returned to our desks. Since it was not the peak time in our project schedule, we could take random breaks at work and have a life while enjoying uninterrupted office conversations. The project was expected to be completed in another 2 weeks.

At around 7 PM, I informed my team lead that I would be taking an off on the next day (Friday), and left for home.

Same Day – 8 PM

"What are you doing?" Gauri asked me. I am not going to tell her about my homecoming. It's a surprise for her.

"Nothing. I will be going out for dinner with Ashish," I responded. My friend Ashish lives in the same apartment building as I do. He stays on the 3rd floor while I live on the 4th.

After dinner, I packed my backpack with enough apparel for 3 days along with some other essential items.

I had booked a cab to take me to the Bengaluru airport at 11.30 PM; it was expected to arrive in another 20 minutes. The airport is about 45 kilometres (30 miles) away from my home, and it would take me around an hour and a half to get there. Hopefully, I would have enough time to check in my luggage and go through security. I had carried a book that I was currently reading as well as an extra one, just in case I finished the current one.

Before leaving home, I reminded myself to put on a mask. With the virus gripping the country and the world, it is important to take precautions. Although very few cases have been found in India, there is a sense of panic as it has just begun to spread across India. The virus is said to be spreading mainly due to the people coming from abroad and airports can be the ideal place for the virus to spread its wings, especially from countries that are already heavily infected.

I reached the airport within the expected time. Surprisingly, only 3 out of 10 people around me were wearing masks. Anyway, I should be taking care of myself.

After checking in my luggage and completing the security check, I reached gate number 23. I was travelling to Indore, a beautiful city in the state of Madhya Pradesh. It is also the nearest airport to my second hometown, Ratlam – 150 km from Indore – and it would take me about 3 hours to get there. I would need to catch a bus from a point that is 15 km from the airport. The travel went as per schedule and I had finished most of the book by the time I reached Ratlam.

I rang the doorbell.

"Please give me Rs. 50," I asked my wife when she opened the door. I was wearing a mask and my face was barely visible. She did not recognize me instantly.

"Prasad? You? Here?" she echoed happily.

"Yeah, this is me, here," I echoed back in the same spirited voice.

"First, give me Rs. 50. I am short of change and need to pay the auto rikshaw driver; he is waiting," I repeated.

After paying the driver, I entered the room and to my surprise, everyone was laughing. It was a pleasant surprise for them.

The next day, my family and me visited one of the palaces nearby, which was built around 150 years ago. It was a white 3-storied structure and was surrounded by huge trees. 2 old bomber weapons were kept on one side of the palace and there was a stable (horse-keeping place) on the other side of the building. Besides this, it also had a couple of other buildings around, which have now been converted into a museum. This museum displayed preserved articles, utensils, equipment, photos, antique vessels and many other items that belonged to kings and queens of the past eras and the Britishers. The museum, however, was not very well managed; a shady smell and the visible dust on the articles did not tell a good story. Nevertheless, the village was very clean and had well-maintained roads. Sometimes a spontaneous trip can prove its worth by showing new places and shades, just like this one – our impromptu history lesson. There was a spectacular cactus garden near the palace – unlike any other place I'd seen before. The huge cactus plants – they may even be called trees – of different species were worth spending time with; each plant had a small board on the front, explaining its origin and speciality. A day well spent came to an end and I slept well that night.

"Have you packed all your belongings?" Gauri asked me the next day morning. She is quite organized complementing her better half's missing trait. I was returning to Bengaluru, alone. My short break would come to an end after spending that entire day at home with her. She wanted to make sure that I had not left anything behind.

"Yeah, looks like I have but I will check once again in the afternoon," I responded.

The flight is at 10 in the night. I would need to take a bus to Indore and then reach the airport by cab, which will be 45 minutes from the bus stop. Somehow, I could manage hire a cab after reaching Indore for airport.

"Why are you wearing a mask?" the cab driver asked while going to airport, to my surprise.

"Just to prevent dust and pollution," I responded, without letting him know that I was a little surprised by his question.

"But Indore does not have much dust. It is very clean and the pollution levels are also very low," he responded, prodding an answer from me while giving me an insight into his apparent knowledge.

"Yeah, you are right but Ratlam wasn't dust-free." I just wanted to put a full stop to his questions. I had been wearing the mask continuously while going to and returning from Ratlam. I did not remove my mask, except when I was home. I felt a little panic setting in as I did not want to become a carrier of the virus and take it back home, nor did I want to contract the virus while travelling back to Bengaluru through the airport, where there may be travellers from outside who are in transit.

"Okay, but remove it while entering the airport. You may get unnecessarily caught while screening," he told me in an informative and suggestive manner. It seemed like he was aware of the situation going on but was still teasing me by asking those questions.

I nodded, showing that I understood his point. However, I was still determined to wear it throughout my travel. I reached Indore around 7 PM, well ahead of time.

While sitting at the gate and waiting for my flight to board, I randomly called up my Jijaji, my elder sister's husband.

"How are you?" I asked.

"I am fine. How are you? Have you reached Indore?" he reciprocated.

"Yeah, at the airport now," I replied quickly.

"Have you seen today's news about the turmoil in the state's politics?" he asked. I had probably missed some recent advancements.

"16 Members of Parliament were sent to a resort and this leader, a stalwart in the state's politics and a part of the state's ruling party, is set to join the opposition. Resort politics is going around," he informed me.

"What? Really? I have been hearing news of him leaving the party for 2 years now due to a rift between the big party leaders, but it seems that day has finally arrived now," I told him.

We talked for some time while I waited for the flight. He managed a pharmaceutical company in Pune city, and being the owner and head of the company, he has mostly been very occupied with work. We like talking with each other and discussing matters around us. He is a cheerful and amiable person with whom I enjoy conversing about various topics. After our chat, I resumed reading again while waiting to board.

I arrived in Bengaluru at midnight and had to wait for an hour for the bus to leave the airport and take me to my destination in the city. I was exhausted and wanted to sleep during the inter-city travel, but the beauty of Bengaluru at night kept me awake. The peaceful and tree-lined roads of the city, which are not often seen during the day, have been my favourite since I first came here 5 years ago. It took about an hour to reach my home, but the time spent watching the city go by on the bus was well worth it.

5.45 AM. The alarm rings.

My daily schedule continues.

It had been 2 to 3 days; the Yoga-Office-Home routine was back to its original pace. Watching the news and following the latest updates was my habit, which I continued doing during working hours as well as at home. An increase in the number of cases across many countries was the topic of every news hour and debate. Everybody was wondering what was going on. Were we not capable enough, even in this advanced age, to come up with a vaccine on time for a virus that was already gulping lives in many advanced countries for over 2 months now? It was spreading fast across the world and the pattern of cases was horrific.

The World Health Organization released daily bulletins, updating all about the situation across the world until one day it was declared "a pandemic."

The next day, I received a message from the Yoga Centre.

"In the wake of coronavirus and the situation, we are closing all activities for the next 15 days. Please wait for further notification."

A well-set routine was going to break from the next day, but a little workout at home and live sessions would make it feasible to stick to it.

Meanwhile, a case or two surfaced in Bengaluru, making noise about the coronavirus. These people had come from abroad and were found to be infected when they developed a few symptoms.

12th March 2020

World Health Organization declared:

"Deeply concerned by the alarming levels of spread. COVID-19 can be characterised as a pandemic."

I found this as the headline almost everywhere when checking the news online. I was doing my usual work in the office and listening to music.

Suddenly, while I was working, the phone rang. It was another friend from a different multinational firm who lived in the neighbourhood. After pausing the music, I answered the call.

"Hey, I am leaving for my hometown," he told me hurriedly.

"Why all of a sudden, all good?" As it was a weekday, I asked why he'd made a sudden decision to leave.

"We have been given the 'Work from Home' option until further notice as a few of the other companies have got some positive coronavirus cases," he explained in a panicked voice.

"Yeah, I am aware of the cases. It is good that you have been asked to work from home. That is a good decision on humanitarian grounds by your company," I reply calmly while thinking of the current situation. I was alone here, far from my family.

Within a few days, a phenomenal number of cases were reported across the country and companies were giving alternatives to their employees. A quarantine leave of 1 to 2 weeks was being given to employees coming from abroad or those arriving from infected countries. In last few days, manufacturing units were cutting down shifts to avoid any mis-happenings.

A slump in the market could be seen arising on a day-to-day basis due to the situation.

Shopping malls were declared closed in almost every part of India.

No gathering of more than 20 people was allowed, anywhere.

Section 144 was imposed in many parts; this meant no gathering of more than 5 people.

International flights to the most infected countries were halted, for an indefinite time. Only rescue flights were allowed to operate from India to those parts of the world.

People were advised not to hide their international travel at all.

People were advised against 'panic buying' to avoid any shortage of daily necessary items.

Hospitals were advised to be on alert and keep their facilities up-to-date.

Guidelines on how to keep homes and premises clean were released.

It was an unusual situation and everything was coming to alert. Were we facing a battleground situation where we were all preparing to fight with an unknown, mini-scale but strong enemy? Industries were going on a standby mode to avoid any further losses. And here we were, making health workers like doctors and nurses, cleaners from town/city municipal corporations and essential goods service providers frontline warriors.

It had been a few days since the cases were increasing but at a turtle's pace – slow and steady in numbers. The cases were of those who had recently come from infected countries and had developed symptoms in 2 to 14 days. Now, all flyers arriving at international airports were asked to be quarantined or isolated for a couple of weeks. While many of the companies had called off work-from-office for many days now, and some since a few weeks, we were still waiting to get it enabled at our workplace. We heard that our company was in full action as they were in the process of analysing the situation to safeguard their employees. For a company that works on developing competitive market products, time-to-market is a key factor. It was tough for them as well to continue work amid such a global situation, ensuring all precautions were taken for their employees.

In the last few days, the company had tried to bring some changes like alternate work from office days, but many of us were still going to the office on a daily basis. In just a couple of days, they started enabling work from home, which had never been a part of the company's policy; it now came as a welcome move. The team lead had been holding short meetings to keep everyone informed about the updates on the situation and the company's forthcoming actions.

22nd March 2020, Sunday

Janta Curfew

Tomorrow is Monday, I must go to the office to enable the laptop and bring it home. I could not do it on Friday due to some or the other work.

A couple of days back, our Prime Minister had declared a 'Janta Curfew' for the entire Sunday, which is today. 'Janta Curfew' means a self-imposed Curfew by the Janta (Public) on themselves. He urged everyone to remain home in order to restrain the coronavirus infection. It is a different matter that he declared it as a request and asked us to implement it by ourselves. Also, he requested the citizens to do a Shankh-naad (the sound of the conch shell as the beginning of our fight against this invisible virus) and give a big cheer to warriors who had already started the fight. There were lakhs of people working in public transportation systems, banks and hospitals, including cleaning staff, grocery store workers and media persons who had been putting themselves at risk to provide their services to others during these panic times, so that basic needs could be served and human lives could be saved. This day was to show our gratitude towards them for their selfless service and symbolise the start of a war for fighting the novel coronavirus.

Probably he wants us to get ready for an even more difficult and challenging situation ahead. Being a responsible citizen and finding it a genuine request, me and Ashish are going on the terrace to do our bit in whatever way possible.

"What do you think is going to happen today?" I chuckle.

"Let us see. He is our Prime Minister and that may be enough for people to listen to him," he sighs while looking around.

And so, it starts. There are sounds of Shankhs – conch shells of ritual and spiritual importance in Hinduism and Buddhism, and Dhols – double-headed drums, bells and clapping coming from all around. Even children are using plates and empty utensils to make noise; by the way, that looks funny but kids seemed to be well entertained.

"We do not have anything with us but we can clap wholeheartedly," I say while clapping.

"Do you know what is the importance of blowing a Shankh?" he asks me.

"Not exactly, but I've heard it creates positive energy," I revert, knowingly.

"Well, that's partly true. The speciality of a Shankh is that the vibrations emanating from blowing it destroy the disease-causing germs in the atmosphere. That is the reason it has an important place in Ayurveda and medicine. I have read it recently," he tries to explain.

"That's nice," I exclaim.

We are happy to help the cause in some way or the other. Although we just clap, it feels good to show our support and appreciate the actions. We get back to our houses quite quickly.

"What are you doing?" I ask Aai. The word 'Aai' means Mother in the Marathi language. She has been a homemaker who loves to prepare food and serve anyone who's visiting home. Despite her age, she is quite tech-savvy and frequently uses social media.

"Just finished chanting. You tell me," she replies calmly. She is also a devout follower of Shri Datta Guru and Lord Shiva and practices daily chanting in the name of God.

"How about father?" I ask her.

"He is outside, ringing the bell enthusiastically. There are many people outside, in the lane in front of our house. It is so loud that I can hear the sounds inside," she says ecstatically.

"Wow, is it? That's nice." I am delighted to hear that he is participating in the activity and enjoying the lively atmosphere. My father is 73 years old and is very active.

It has been 13 years since he retired, but still dresses up in crisp ironed clothes every day and stays active by doing a variety of outdoor activities. It makes me reflect on my own laziness and motivates me to try to match his exuberance.

After some chat and food, I jump back to reading my current book.

Time is passing by with the same routine. Considering the current situation, during one of our talks my sister asked, "Why don't you come to Pune? You can reach here quickly."

"A little due to the panic as many flyers from abroad will be travelling around and I do not want to be a carrier, breaking into your house," I explain my concern.

"I would be travelling home via Nagpur by road or air as soon as possible so that I can be with our parents," I added. My hometown, Betul, is situated in the Satpura Valley, which is known for its dense forests and curved ghats. This beautiful town is surrounded by hills from all sides.

Although she asks me to move to her place a couple of times, I decline the offer. By this time, the number of positive cases in Pune has become higher than any other metro city and that is worrisome.

All international flyers arriving in India are already getting screened at airports and a small percentage are found to be infected. There is panic-flying from abroad into India, which also brings domestic flying under suspicion.

Travel by bus or train has already become suspicious due to the irresponsible behaviour of a few people. Many flyers coming from infected countries were stamped on their hands and asked to stay under quarantine or isolation after being screened upon arrival. These passengers have been found migrating from one place to the other in trains and buses and were caught after information was provided by fellow passengers.

The next day in the office, everyone looks like they are in a panic situation. Many have come and are updating their systems with the required software for work-from-home conditions.

"How long will you be here?" I ask a colleague and friend.

"Another couple of hours. Just want to ensure the system is up," he replies while doing his work.

"Yeah, this should work at home but if it does not, what can we do?" I giggle, hinting at the tragic point.

It will not be easy for the IT department to get everything up and working seamlessly in a home setup. Like many of the other companies, ours too is enabling it for the very first time, and as an employee, I can understand the depth of effort required.

Me and my friend both leave together after some silly hiccups while carrying our work laptops from the office to home.

Part II: 1.0

A Tough Decision

With your basket and my basket the people will live

– Māori Proverb

Day 0: It Begins

Today: Tuesday, 24th March 2020

Time: 7.30 PM

Today is the first day I have worked from home. It has been quite seamless. I am thinking of heading back to my hometown soon and start checking out options to leave as soon as I can. Internet connectivity is good almost everywhere, including my hometown. If this situation prevails for many days, at least I will be with family.

The coronavirus is spreading across the country, though at the same turtle's pace. The Prime Minister is going to give a speech at 8 this evening – about half an hour from now.

Ashish has come home and as we sit in my living room, we are thinking about what's going to happen next.

We are in front of the television, holding cups of the delightful 'Green tea with lemon honey'. I prepared it well; this I can brag about now as Ashish – who is not fond of green tea thinking it makes him vomit, which he has actually done earlier – has found it potable.

"So, how is it working from home?" he asks.

"Quite good, apart from some silly hurdles. I was not expecting it to be this smooth," I reply.

"That's good."

"How about you?" I ask back.

"We've already been working from home for the last 10 to 12 days now. I went to the office today to check some hardware boards," he explained.

"Okay, that is nice. Now you are free to go back to Mumbai. When are you planning to leave?" I ask.

"Let's see, maybe soon," he replies in short.

"Our PM's call to the nation is about to begin. It is not the first time that the PM is calling the nation in any situation though," I giggle.

"But this time, there seem to be some serious circumstances. Global health organizations have declared a pandemic and his speech is what all Indians are looking forward to," I add, expressing my concern to him. I am hoping we will be with our families soon.

PM's Call to the Nation – 8 PM

"India will be under a complete lockdown starting midnight today."

"This is like a curfew and will be far stricter than the 'Janata Curfew' held on 22nd March (a day before)."

"To stop this virus, stay at a distance from each other and better stay inside your houses......"

And it continues.

"If we don't handle these next 21 days well, then our country and your family will go backwards by 21 years."

"Stay Inside Your Homes. Stay Safe."

Alas...

When our PM, with folded hands, is requesting our countrymen to stay inside their homes to safeguard themselves from the virus, it is not difficult to imagine just how catastrophic a decision it's been for him as well as for every citizen.

India is facing a steady increase in the number of positive cases that have started appearing in various cities across the country.

Though the television has been called an idiot box in the modern era, it has nonetheless served well to the millions of introverts, who do not like talking or interacting with real people around but will be profusely happy to stick to the television cabinet, listening to characters, just like an acquiescent child is ready to listen to their mother.

It has served well even in recent times to broadcast speeches, live sports matches, calls to the nation by nation heads, events, national and international news as well as various forms of entertainment.

"The operations of scheduled domestic commercial airlines shall cease effective midnight, that is 23.59 hours IST on 24th March 2020 – today." A 'Breaking News' flashes on the screen.

We stop talking for a while. There is silence amid the news anchor's announcement and the boomerang background music.

"What!!" I yell, breaking the silence in a heavy voice.

"There seems to be a difficult situation ahead and a tough decision has been taken by the PM," Ashish says with a sigh.

The sudden thought of not being able to visit my family amid the current panic situation makes me feel helpless and troubled. The thought that I can't do anything to help them during this time keeps bothering me. 21 days is not a small duration, and looking at the situation of the other countries, would it be possible to have a lockdown of just 21 days? Can it go on for longer than this duration?

There is another round of silence at home but my mind is in a state of tremendous chaos, as I'm sure is his.

The situation will remain the same until 14th April.

No normal movement for people anywhere, including between villages, towns, cities or metros.

No passenger flights.

No passenger trains running on the tracks.

No buses plying the roads.

No restaurants are open and malls have already been closed for many days now.

No temples/mosques/churches or any religious places to be open for gathering.

No offices are to be open, except banks or top government centres.

No school/college exams; they have already been closed for many days now.

The idea is to contain the virus and restrict the movement of people who can become carriers and spread it exponentially. I got to know that we are in the 2nd phase of the pandemic, wherein the virus can spread only from an infected person arriving from an infected country – an imported case. The 3rd stage begins when person-to-person transmission of the virus starts within a community.

"Why did you come back from Mumbai or did not go back sooner?" I turn to Ashish and ask.

"There was some issue in the office and I was called back. But it now looks like I am stuck," he says with regret.

The lockdown continues...

Days are passing at home. I start with a little exercise and yoga in the morning, continue office work around the clock and take out some time in between to prepare and eat food while watching the news at times. A famous and old television channel has started re-running epic shows like 'Ramayana' and 'Mahabharata', apart from a few others of different genres. I was a small kid when these shows were aired for the first time, years back. Their decision to re-telecast these mythology series is extremely welcoming during this lockdown as they are more like childhood favourites of millions of Indians. A society that boosts traditions and cultures with a lot of festivals has now been forced behind closed walls. In this scenario, an hour or two of watching the inspiring life stories of Lord Rama and Lord Krishna can help reduce negativity and enhance morale.

Indians are largely following the restrictions imposed but there is news coming from some parts of India where people are ignoring the lockdown, roaming the streets and arranging gatherings. There are countries that are facing the consequences of either not imposing a lockdown or enforcing it late or even totally ignoring it. China is already at its peak in terms of the number of cases and deaths. Many countries like the USA, Italy, Germany and Spain are trailing close behind. All countries are trying to contain the situation and keep their people safe. Every day, there are advisories to be at home, keep washing hands and use sanitisers if in contact with others or touching public objects.

Day 7: Outbreak in India

Breaking News:

"Migrants are stranded at many locations across India amid the pandemic outbreak."

"Stranded migrants are being screened and getting deported to their hometowns."

"All migrants are either kept in quarantine in temporary shelters or at home."

"These people should get help soon. It is not their mistake; they cannot help but move in such times," I echo. They are daily wage earners or workers from mills and factories that are now closed due to the lockdown.

Due to the panic and deprivation of basic needs, these migrants are desperately trying to move back to their hometowns in the fear of losing their hard-earned money by paying rents needlessly, when they are not earning. They are scattered on the roads and are using any possible means they have like bicycles, bullock carts, tractors, trolleys or bikes. These heart-wrenching visuals have shaken the capital of India as well as the entire country.

Few more highlights on the news:

"Migrants gather in large numbers in the outskirts of New Delhi, the capital of India."

"Thousands of people have been stranded on the roads for more than 12 hours and are trying to get help."

Many are seen walking towards their homes with their luggage and others are using bullock carts and tractors to reach their hometowns along with their close aides. It seemed like a nightmare that should have never been true.

This kind of crowd can elevate the situation to any level and bring distress to their near and dear ones if they get infected.

The scenario has stayed the same for a couple of days now. Hats off to the officials, doctors and police personnel who are working tirelessly to bring control and stability to this situation. The Chief Minister of Uttar Pradesh, the state that is most impacted due to these migrants, is actively monitoring the situation and has arranged for hundreds of buses for these migrants. The same is being followed by several other states as well. In the next few days, although the situation may not be completely evicted, it looks like it will come under control.

Over the next few days, I have resisted watching the news as it brings out a sense of sadness in me. The world is nowhere close to recovering and India is raining cases too. Also, the office work is at another level; I have got enough work to keep myself busy for many hours.

"I am not able to connect to the system. I've been trying to connect for the last 1 hour," someone in our office group pinged on Messenger.

"Yeah, me too. I'm stuck at the last stage and am not able to connect," another claimed.

From the first day itself, though it has not been this seamless for the others, I have never faced any issues while connecting to the remote system. I believe exaggeration has no limitations and have seen it many times during the last few days.

While I am usually working throughout the day, I tend to reserve my afternoon breaks for preparing food and eating as I continue working. A casual walk towards late evening or at night on the terrace of my apartment makes me feel better and connected.

"What have you prepared today, Prasad?" Aai calls to ask.

"Veg Pulav in the house today," I reply. "I have never been a good cook but I can say this lockdown will bring out the cook in me," I continue, chuckling.

"Definitely," she says, laughing.

Ashish comes home around 7 in the evening as we have got into the habit of walking on the terrace for at least an hour every day now. We need to have some activity that will help us refresh our body and mind; for us, it is walking and talking in the evening or at night, as and when time permits.

"Would you like some jaggery tea?" I ask.

"Okay, that sounds cool," he nods.

"I have taken sugar out from my diet and you, being a first-stage diabetic, a cup of jaggery tea would be a good option to control your sugar level," I chuckle. Ashish laughs.

The tea is ready and it seems it has turned out quite good.

"Okay. I have given one utility run in my office work and want to ensure it finishes off without any issues. It will take about 20 minutes, then we can go to the terrace."

"Yeah, that's fine," he replies.

"You can surf news channels or something else till then," I say, handing the remote to him.

"How did you get into this industry, Prasad? I mean, what motivated you and since when are you working here?" Ashish suddenly pops these questions after a few minutes of scanning the channels.

Usually, Ashish and I talk about topics like the current situation, politics, work and life. This time, it is a question from the past. He probably thinks it's a good way to pass the time while the run is finishing.

I chuckle and take a deep breath, exhaling slowly so that it may appear like I'm avoiding the question.

"Right now, even if I am the son of my loving parents, a husband to my dear wife, a close friend for a few, an acquaintance for many others and a pygmy engineer for a corporate giant, I have been a typical middle-class boy who was average in studies. I am currently working in a world-known firm, and what could be more satisfactory than one working in his dream job? A job, which one has dreamt of since childhood. Though we never stop dreaming, sometimes it feels like a milestone and at many times it feels like nothing..." I start telling him my story after switching off the volume of the the TV.

"It may not be that interesting and might seem like a story of every house. While this is right, let me pull you into a flashback."

We continue our chit-chat while sipping on the tea.

"Whenever a growing me, in short pants, looked around at working people, I would think of becoming like them. Seeing some good option, I would instantly take a liking to it, making it a dream, if not for many days then a few at least. For every kid, apart from his mother and father, there can be a lot of heroes around him/her, which he/she never admits to. For example, seeing heroism in the people who work in the field that the kid has taken a liking to. I was no different."

"No wonder everyone is a hero in their society:

A Teacher – A respective figure, a kid's early days mentor, punisher and caretaker, with whom he spends most time during his school days. Here, heroism flourishes.

A Carpenter – The guy doing artistic woodwork.

An Engineer – Almost every Indian middle-class parent's dream for their kid. The kid also sees it as a secure future option for him/her.

A Doctor – Almost every doctor's dream is for their kid to go on and become a doctor. He is someone's 'God' who helps them get a restart in life when they facing the toughest of times with their health.

A Shopkeeper – This hero gives chocolates to every kid, that too of his choice, for a few cents and keeps serving the neighbourhood for years to come.

An Electrician – Someone who waves a magical wand and fixes any electric issues at home.

And many more…" I continue speaking after taking a few more sips of the tea.

"However, I was later most impressed by one of these heroes, which remained with me forever. Around 20 years back, televisions used to come in the form of cabinets and had to be mandatorily placed on a mid-sized table. Apart from colour, they were in black and white pictures too. Whenever there was an issue with the functioning of the TV, a sophisticated person would come to the house, open this plastic box and fix the problem by melting some points and joining others, to bring the cabinet back to life. Those small tracks, miniatures of building-like shapes and metal traces like roads created a city-like structure behind the display. I found it beyond magical and mysterious; this magician was called a technician. I became an ardent fan of his and thought he was amazing. I believed this person had a magic wand, but also wondered how he did it.

Unaware of the actual work that this technician does, I was highly attracted to the concept and decided what to become when I grew up. Nevertheless, this dream got converted or may have been diverted into becoming an engineer but with the same focus, just to do magical work with electronic instruments. As you know, in those days, a growing kid from a middle-class family could think of multiple dream jobs, but may finally end up becoming an engineer – this was the reality. The more the kid is from an average-doing family, the more are his chances of becoming an engineer, back then," I say, laughing.

While I was completely pulled back to those old days, I tried to get back to the present and continue.

"Today, when I am working as a Chip Design Engineer for a multinational firm and doing my dream job, I understand the joints and points that the technician used to melt and fix. The magic wand that the technician used, which seemed to be beyond the capability of that kid, is now in his hands. I have been contributing to developing those small pieces of several electronic instruments or appliances – Integrated Circuits in a variety of products. It is a dream come true and is continuing."

"Did you ever think of coming so far away for your bread and butter, then?" he asks curiously.

"Thinking of coming this far? Never. I was not even aware of what to do with my life after becoming an engineer. Forget about coming this far. Now, I always wonder if is it even worth it to stay a thousand miles away from my parents and hometown, losing my close childhood friends. Though I have made a few new friends here, in Bengaluru, things will never be that way."

"Well, that is true. It is the same situation for many guys out there. I also think that way sometimes. After all, leaving Mumbai has been not easy for me as well," he adds.

"How about you? Being a Mumbaikar (resident of Mumbai City) and coming to Bengaluru?" I curiously ask him.

"Well, you seem to be a storyteller and I may not do justice with the flow," he chuckles.

"Hey, just tried my bit and kept the pages open. So, tell me your journey so far," I ask as I keep the empty cup aside.

"Nobody wants to leave Mumbai once you start living there, and I have been there since my childhood. No wonder it is called the city of dreams," he chuckles and continues.

"I came to Bengaluru around 7 and a half years ago. I was working in the non-technical field in Mumbai before joining the IT industry here. I started my software journey with a small firm and gradually took an interest in Linux core development. Now, being a part of a top Linux core development company itself is a different feeling. As you said, being from a typical middle-class family, I was also dreaming of becoming an engineer and completed my post-graduate diploma in software development from Pune. Later, I found myself in my field of interest."

"Well, that is excellent. Never thought of going back to Mumbai again all this while?" I ask.

"I sometimes do think about it but the lack of opportunities in my field of work in Mumbai makes me stick to this city. I am the eldest child of a joint family and have been fortunate enough to get settled quite well. Hence, a lot of responsibilities fall on me. I tell you, it is a good and strangely sad feeling at the same time. I belong to a community in Uttar Pradesh, a Northern part of India, and am still connected to the big family in all aspects," he gives me a brief of his family connection and continues.

"My father usually reminds me of one saying: 'Even if you feel exhausted when helping someone from the family or any friends, remember, do not go that far where you are alone and have nothing left.' So, I have quite a bigger role to play at various times. Once my parents and wife shift here, to Bengaluru, the situation will be much better."

"Well, that's very true," I say with an affirmative look.

"I get you. I also belong to a joint family and I believe everyone has responsibilities, more or less in any circumstances," I respond, trying to be sensible.

"Well, you said you are a post-graduate diploma holder, right? Which institute did you certify from?" I continue.

To this, he replies with the name of the institute and we realise that we are a part of the same institute; same batch but different centres, and we had never talked about this so far, until now. It is a small world, after all. We never knew until this time and have figured it out just now. Discussions continue on our experiences there and many other topics as we browse through channels.

Suddenly, we see breaking news on the television with visuals that are quite disturbing.

"Around 6000 people had gathered for a religious ceremony during the 3rd week of March in New Delhi."

"2500 people are still present inside one building, under one roof."

"People from 16 countries visited and many left for other destinations within the country."

"People travelled to many states using trains, buses and flights to reach this gathering held on 23rd March."

"Death of a person in Hyderabad unfolded the mystery, and tracing the patient's whereabouts brought this event to light."

And it continues.

"Since afternoon, people are being screened for symptoms and are instructed to go into quarantine or isolation. Those found positive in the tests are being admitted into hospitals."

There have been a few incidents of ignoring the lockdown but this is horrific. This is the first incident when people – from India and abroad – gathered in large numbers and then went on to many other places, knowingly or unknowingly. This is scary to imagine; the chain that we Indians are trying to break in order to stop the spread of this virus may now grow even more!

"This is insane. These kinds of guys will never help the well-being of society. Why the hell can't they understand the gravity of the situation?" I am furious.

"Really! Many innocent citizens might have to pay heavily for this. Be it their own community or others who might have travelled with them or come in contact. God forbid, if even 10% of them are infected, what would be the situation in the coming days?" Ashish says angrily.

After getting to know more about the incident, we found that the people had gathered from several countries, including those that were barred. People were asked to go into quarantine or isolation once they arrived from these countries. The head of this gathering was missing and the police had lodged a case against him. VISA companies were being traced and banned if found guilty; foreigners were being deported or quarantined. Officials, who could not find this happening under their noses, were being questioned.

In India, the cases have been increasing rapidly every day. A significant percentage of the positive cases were of those who had attended the gathering of a certain section of society in New Delhi. All the burden was on the frontline warriors – the police, doctors, nurses and social workers. The police had started tracing the contacts, finding them, screening them, forcing them to stay inside their homes for quarantine or isolation and helping to admit them into hospitals, if found infected. This action may not prevent the consequences but may help in containing it. When those ignorant people have travelled to other places and their homes, their families as well as the people around them are at risk. I wondered why they were hiding and why they could not come out since the lockdown was announced.

The cases are rapidly increasing in many countries and the number of deaths seems to be following the pattern. It has been a week now since international and domestic flights were stopped. Except for essential services, all modes of transport have been halted. The market has fallen like never before in the last two decades. All shops are closed except for 1 or 2 grocery/vegetable stores within the vicinity of 2 to 3 km. There are a few circles drawn in front of each shop and people have been asked to stay inside those circles while standing in the queue. Roads are empty, without any curfew in the country. The visuals are frightening and the experience is spine-chilling. Usually, only a war can have this sort of an impact at so many levels, but this time it is a micrometre-sized virus that has done it.

Life & Rebirth

Although it is small, it is greenstone

– Māori Proverb

Day 11: Seed to Sprout

It has been 10 days since people are locked in their houses. When I start my day with the daily routine of light yoga and some exercise, it fills me with positivity.

Listening to classical instrumental music, whenever I feel like it, is a part of my day in the morning, afternoon and evening. Immersing myself in the soul of instruments like the flute, santoor and tabla makes me feel rejuvenated. And doing yoga with these classics playing in the background is a feeling of a different level. Whether I'm doing office work or personal work or writing my own thoughts down, these instruments have been my constant companion for a few days now.

Suddenly, during one of my morning yoga sessions, the phone rings.

"What are you doing?" asks my wife from the other side.

She has been feeling a little uneasy and has had a backache since morning. She is still in her hometown.

Last night too, she was feeling the same, but felt better later and could sleep well.

We are in our 9th month of pregnancy and these are probably signs of the start of labour. It is said that along with the woman, her better half also gets pregnant; however; I would say it's the woman who should get all the credit for new life. God has given most blessings to women, who are able to give birth and get rebirth. We, as men, can never match a woman's glory.

A sudden tsunami of feelings strikes my shore of thoughts. I am not there with her at this moment. I cannot leave my place. There may have been many births during this lockdown, but I would have never thought that on the day it would be my turn, I would be so helpless.

I think of those army men who are on the field all the time to protect us and guard the country. They are not able to be with their families in so many difficult or good times. I am in the same situation as the world grapples with the pandemic. Everyone who is staying in their houses and not playing with the fire outside is saving lives. I got to know about many doctors who are not going back home so that they do not infect their own family members, even by mistake. There are chances that even a healthy person can be a carrier of the virus, if they act irresponsibly.

"Everything will be alright." Your heart speaks a lot to yourself when you are alone. I am not with my parents, so I just talk to them to feel 'okay' and calm myself down.

God has created a situation wherein my parents also cannot travel to see my wife and be with her. Gauri's family is with her now, which is probably what she needs the most.

While talking to my wife and second family there, I have given quite a few instructions, as if they do not know anything. They are a caring family and can handle any situation well.

Many of my friends and known people, who work in other companies, have reached their hometowns well in time or just before the lockdown was declared.

I am here in Bengaluru, with nowhere to go. Stuck in the lockdown like several other Indians. It has been almost 10 days now; I have not gone out except once, to purchase groceries and veggies.

Around 7 in the evening:

"Shall we go for a walk on the terrace?" Ashish messages me.

"Yeah, let's go in 5 mins," I respond.

The climate is indeed very nice. There is a gentle breeze blowing and the trees are enjoying the cool wind as if they are very happy with the pollution-free environment of the last few days. It is a very positive and energetic feeling to be in such a climate.

At around 7.40 PM the phone rings. It's my wife's mother on the other side.

"Congratulations!! It is a baby boy," she announces happily.

A broad smile spreads on my face and I experience a deep sense of being the happiest person in the world, yet a little emotional inside, which I must hide for now.

"Wow, congratulations to you too!"

She has also become a grandmother.

"When and what time? I just spoke to Gauri a couple of hours back," I ask.

"The doctor had called us for a check-up at around 7 PM and immediately asked to get her into the OPD. Within 10 minutes, we heard the crying of a baby but thought it might be someone else as she had just got in. They brought the baby to us right now, after cleaning the newborn. Both mother and baby are completely fine," she gives me all the information in detail.

I felt relaxed as if I was right there with them.

"How is Gauri?" I enquire again, to which she replies that she is doing well and is in the room, taking rest.

I am very happy. Yeah, of course, I am a proud father now.

A quick hug from Ashish, whom I am walking with on the terrace, makes me more emotional.

I call my mother. "What are you doing, Aaji?"

As soon as I say that, she senses my happy voice on the phone call. 'Aaji' is grandmother in Marathi.

"Wow, what time?" she asks immediately.

I give her all the details that I received over the phone from my mother-in-law.

"Please give this news to Baba," I request her.

"Of course, I'll tell him right away," she replies. I get emotional and cut the call.

After a few minutes, I call back and try to talk in a calm voice so that she does not sense my happy emotional tone. "Yeah, the call dropped. I will call others and get back to you later."

Though this is tremendously happy news, I have been feeling like a caged person who cannot help or be with his family in this situation. I have been talking to Gauri over the phone and on video calls. She may be feeling that I should have been there with her but is not expressing it openly. However, I cannot help it.

"How are you feeling, proud father?" Ashish asks.

"Very happy and emotional," I reply joyfully.

"Do not worry, you will be seeing him soon," he says as he senses my eagerness to see my newborn son.

It is an indescribable feeling when you are far away and unable to be present in the moment. A tsunami of thoughts floods my mind and I wonder what it would be like if I was there with them. If things were different, I could have seen my new champion and his mother, and held the baby in my arms to cuddle and admire.

"How are you, Atya (Aunt)?" I call my sister.

Without any delay, she guesses the news and asks back in a happy voice, "Wow, what time? How are the mother and baby?" I give her all the details and we talk for some time.

A message notification brought before me the most beautiful sight I have ever seen in my lifetime so far: the first image of my newborn baby. He is incredibly handsome, with his closed yet beautiful eyes that are adorned with long lashes and light eyebrows above them. He has reddish cheeks, small hands with long fingers and a small, adorable nose. He is wrapped in a blue dress provided by the hospital. I stare lovingly at him, my heart full of love.

"The baby was shivering when the nurse brought him out to show us, so she immediately took him inside to keep him warm and for a check-up," I am told on a call that I got some time back. I was worried but calmed down when they explained that everything was fine now.

I returned home with a sense of thankfulness to the Almighty for taking care of Gauri and the baby. It has been an hour now. I have called all my close people and messaged many more. I have just been on phone calls since the news broke out; after all, everyone deserves a bit of good news considering the present scenario.

I thank God for this day and for everything till today.

Today, our PM has requested the citizens of India to shut off their lights at 9 PM for 9 minutes and light diyas, candles or torches in support of the warriors. We must show support to all our frontline warriors with #9pm9minutes. This may look absurd, but yes, warriors like doctors, nurses, policemen, cleaning staff of municipal corporations, vegetable suppliers and grocery store owners, who keep their shops open so that people can have access to their basic needs, as well as bank officials and many social workers from all sections of the society – they are truly showing warriorship and the strength of humanity. They deserve to be supported and shown the strength of being one united nation. They also have families waiting for them to return home safely.

Ashish comes down and suggests another walk on the terrace. It is 8.58 PM. I wrap up my work and we quickly go up with one torch, after switching off all the lights in the house. I am constantly on calls for the good news I have got today. We do not have diyas, so we light the torch and flash our mobiles. This is the time when we should support our warriors like we do during war times. After all, this is a war – one where everyone is on the battlefield along with the frontline warriors. The rest of us are contributing to this war by being at home, not going out, keeping social distancing and using adequate precautions to safeguard ourselves and those around us. People at home and in the buildings around us are seen to be supporting the cause. Lights inside their houses are off and they are on their terraces or balconies with diyas, torches or candles. There are fireworks also at a few places. Hope they are following the protocol of maintaining social distancing. We come back inside in about 15 minutes.

I have forgotten my hunger. Ashish and I thought we would eat the same pulav that I had made that afternoon. We must just heat it up first. However, I am not able to do so because of continuous incoming calls.

"Prasad, where is oil and the other ingredients for making noodles? We can have it along with the pulav," Ashish suggests.

I try helping him find all the ingredients he needs, and he starts preparing the noodles. I am still on calls.

"Congratulations!! How are you feeling?" I ask my wife in a happy voice.

"Yeah, fine now. Congratulations to you too," she replies softly and we talk for a few minutes.

Recently, I got to know about a lady doctor in Pune, India, who has been actively engaged in developing indigenous self-testing kits for the coronavirus. She delivered a baby and on the next day, she delivered the test kits to India.

"My responsibilities are to serve the people first, everything comes second," she mentioned in an interview. I feel a sense of pride while going through this news feed.

Later, Ashish and I have our dinner and he leaves for home, just one floor down.

After some time, I get a call, informing me about the well-being of my wife and child. They are back in their private room. Gauri is feeling tired, of course; it is not easy giving birth, after all.

Another photo of my baby boy surfaces. He has reddish cheeks, beautiful black eyes that are slightly open, a little less dense but silky hair, small hands with long fingers and a sharp popping nose.

For the rest of the hours of that night, I was on continuous calls and messages until late at night. "May God bless our baby and all other newborns who are born in this situation across the world." An emotional thought floats in my mind as I finally go to bed.

A couple of days have passed with the same routine of working from home, preparing food, eating, sleeping and walking on the terrace. Apart from that, I now have one extra task that I look forward to the most. Calling my wife and asking her about our little tomato. I know I am disturbing every person there, calling and asking every hour and wondering if they have taken pictures of the baby so that they can share them.

The baby is sleeping every now and then. Whenever I make video calls, he is either sleeping or looking around with one or another eye open. I have still not got to see both his eyes open. Gauri is completely fine and gradually recovering from the aftereffects of delivery.

"Some newborns sleep for like 20 to 21 hours. Later, after 2 to 3 months, they will not let you sleep as they sleep during the day and are wide awake at night," Aai told me during one of our calls.

After 48 hours of birth, I am seeing a few more pictures of the baby.

Cases are still on the rise in India. Almost 500 to 600 cases are being added on a daily basis. The count of those deceased is more than a hundred now and the government is trying to get a hold of the situation. They are trying to control the situation with every possible effort and are working for the more vulnerable sections of society who should be kept away from this pandemic, otherwise, the situation will be grave. In India, the pandemic is still under control and the numbers have been contained to a certain extent since the first case was reported. Around the world, around 190 countries have been caught by this deadly virus and the total cases are now touching 1.5 million, with the deceased count reaching 80,000. The situation is getting very difficult for everyone on earth. Developing nations are struggling and developed nations are trying to put in the best possible efforts to get rid of the situation. There is news of a shortage of isolation beds and ventilators, even in developed countries. A vaccine is under development and may need another 15 months to complete testing on humans.

The Curious Case of Hotspots

Day 20

This is day 20 of the lockdown and most of the citizens have not stepped out except to buy essentials. I too went out last week – just the 2nd time in these 20 days – to buy the essentials that were needed. The nearest grocery store is hardly 200 meters from my home, so it does not worry me much and it's easy to come back within a short time.

The world is seeing a huge surge in active cases, spreading across many countries. It is reaching a 2 million count, while as many as a lakh have passed away; this number is still increasing by thousands every day. In the past 15 days, the USA has become the new epicentre of the pandemic apart from countries like Italy and Spain.

Many of them, the so-called first-world countries, are now in stage 3 of the pandemic – community transmission. In this stage, the infection spreads from person to person within the community. Due to this, the cases are growing in number.

In India, the number of positive cases has crossed 10,000 and more than 300 are deceased. Today, more than 1200 positive cases have been reported. There are many hotspots where the number of cases is higher. Mumbai is seeing more than a thousand, while almost all metro and semi-metro cities now have more than 300 positive cases. Around 2 lakh tests are being conducted across the country. The central government is putting tremendous efforts into increasing the tests across India so that positive cases can be unfolded and the situation can be contained. Many state governments have declared hotspots in their respective states and these zones will be completely shut down, even after 14th April, when the 21 days – 3 weeks – are completed. These hotspots will remain under lockdown until 30th April. This is to prevent cases from increasing uncontrollably.

Majorly affected states have already declared an extension of the lockdown and some have announced relaxation in the areas where the cases are less than 5. Zero-case districts/areas may see industries reopening from 15th April and may also start some transportation to the adjoining districts that are also without cases. Boundaries will remain sealed among the districts/states that are still at high risk and are declared hotspots. One statement from the central government states that the cases would have been close to half a million if the lockdown had not been imposed, or much higher than what we have right now if the lockdown had not been followed to this extent.

Tomorrow will be the 21st day of this 1st phase of the lockdown, and in the morning, at 10 AM our PM will be delivering a call to the nation. A couple of days back, the PM had a video conference with the Chief Ministers of all the states and union territories. A few ministers could not hold the water in their stomachs and have leaked the information that they have all agreed to extend the lockdown. This may lead to panic and additional movement of migrants and other people. Statements like these should be given with all readiness to prevent their consequences.

Since the last 20 days, my day-to-day routine has settled and my body's biological clock has adapted to the new way of living. Every day after office hours, once work is completed, it is time for a walk.

"Are you going to book a flight? Not that bookings are open yet," Ashish asks me a couple of days later, while we are walking on the terrace.

"Yeah, but I do not think the lockdown is getting over anytime soon. Also, the situation is not good in either Nagpur or Indore," I respond with concern over the continuing situation. These 2 cities are the nearest airports to my hometown and my wife's place.

"Our champ completed a week yesterday, right?"

"Yeah, I remember it well. A week back, we were on the terrace, taking a walk, when the good news came." He reminds me of those moments.

I wonder when I will get to see him for the first time and take him in my arms. When will I be able to touch his soft, small hands and feet? I am deep in thought for a quick moment.

"Yeah," I just sigh and pause for an instant.

"Anyways, what I am thinking is that the lockdown isn't going to end anytime soon."

I picked the topic we were discussing a while back. Ashish is least interested in discussing the pandemic situation. He always says that these depressing talks are of no use, just a waste of time.

"I feel like I'm living in a Hollywood movie," I say, trying to steer the conversation in a funny way.

"Yeah, that is quite true. Quite a panic situation around and everyone is afraid," he laughs.

"What if we become zombies due to the virus infection?" I let my imagination run wild.

"Hunting for people or groceries," he says, trying to carry it forward.

"We as zombies would chase and hunt the people. People are anyways hunting for groceries due to the lack of essentials," I try to give wings to my imagination.

"Oh, my bad God, even he will fear," Ashish laughs out loud again.

"And I will start my hunt from the office; I'll take everyone on one by one. I am a mutant of the highest grade and cannot be killed by any bullet or weapon," I add to the story, making it even more horrible.

"Hey, wait, wait," Ashish roars in horror. "Now you are scaring the hell out of me. Are you all fine?" he asks in concern and then chuckles.

Laughing out of my mind, I notice his concern and tell him that I am absolutely fine. I ask him not to worry; this is just a way of easing out my worries. I had a similar discussion at length with one of my friends when the infection started in our country.

With regard to this conversation on the terrace, I have penned down a blog. Some of the paragraphs are cited below:

"This century has created a monster out of a human being, who is claiming the throne on earth by harvesting the environment. We are exploiting nature, which we rarely think of conserving. In the name of environment conservation, a few try to spread the message through photo ops, politics and articles, but nothing solid has come out of it. Is it now time for nature to fight and take on human beings?

There is currently one category of hotspots in this world and these are the zones where the coronavirus cases are present in huge numbers. Another category of hotspots, which claimed to be the face of the growing economic world, are the gigantic industrial cities that are close to a shutdown.

With the developments in this century, we are thinking of ourselves as being on top of the world and harvesting nature for our luxuries, as per our necessities. Huge factories, industrial plants, billions of vehicles and many advanced machineries, created by humans, are now in existence on earth. The world is facing the consequences and many of the species are either extinct or on the verge of extinction due to polluted air, water and soil.

No wonder, with this lockdown, many countries including India are seeing an increase in the quality of air and water, and lesser pollution due to the shutdown of factories and plants in the last couple of months. No smoke omission from manufacturing units and no traffic on city roads has led to much better air quality as compared to the pre-lockdown times. No industrial waste and zero waste thrown into the rivers have led to cleaner waters everywhere. And this change in the climate can be felt and seen visibly, everywhere.

Long Live Mother Earth! Long Live Her Kingdom!"

Day 21

"It is no time to play chess when the house is on fire."

– An Italian Proverb

"We will continue the lockdown till 3rd May with the same seriousness and even more strictness."

"The country has enough stock of medicines and ration. Hurdles in the supply chain are constantly being addressed. We are also moving forward rapidly in the field of health infrastructure."

"Keeping in mind the livelihoods of our poor brothers and sisters, provisions of limited relaxations in identified places, starting from 20th April, have been made. Daily wagers and those who depend on daily earnings are my family."

"In case of any positive development in any area or district, we can give conditional concessions from April 20th. In case of any violation or the development of any new hotspots, these concessions will be rolled back in those areas."

These words from the PM shook me again. I have been following the situation all these days and was aware that an extension of the lockdown looked inevitable. Yet I believed that if it opened up, I would be able to fly off to see my newborn, and sooner or later, go back to my hometown. It seemed like it was bound to happen, and here we are now, in the 2nd phase of the lockdown. Few tweets followed the PM's speech and in no time from the opposition leaders for not shutting down the country on time, declaring lockdown suddenly and not arranging food for the poor and marginalised community. Of course, this should have happened and that should be happening, these are all speculative statements. We can say it anytime as there is always scope for criticism in whatever one does. It is about timing, and probably, we have shut down at the right time. 21 days are good enough to make some impact. Migrant issues seem to be based on rumours that the police must deal with, as well as with those who are spreading these lies when they should be utilizing their authority and power for the good of society.

I have been reading about the Emergency declared between 1975 to 1977, for around 21 months, and the grieving situation of that time. It was proposed by the then PM and issued by the President. I have read about the detentions, censoring of the press and how civil liberties were suspended. A government can declare such an emergency only during a natural disaster, civil unrest, armed conflict, situation of war, medical pandemic or epidemic or other biosecurity risks. I learnt from available resources that there was no such thing as a valid reason, then.

This lockdown is not yet an emergency, although it has been declared a pandemic by the World Health Organization. Print media is the 4th pillar of democracy and they have been contributing immensely during this time. They are like the frontline warriors, helping Indians know more about the virus and its symptoms, taking stock of the situation and making everyone in every city, area and country aware of it. Essential services are seemingly on track in tier-1 and tier-2 cities. Everyone there is getting what they need delivered to their doorstep as they have the much-needed infrastructure like a few apps and the necessary ecosystem around it, along with the UPI payment system. No-contact delivery is a no-talk, no-connect kind of delivery culture that is taking precedence in the very busy lives of working people. Mid-tier cities might be gearing up for the same; as India is an IT hub, it can probably still build this ecosystem in no time. However, small cities and villages, which have different ecosystems wherein people themselves mobilise a lot for their daily needs and connect with each other, are seemingly less active and facing issues in the availability of daily essentials due to the supply-chain disruption, where most of the supply comes from the nearest big city. Banks are open with utmost precautions, only for required services.

"How is quarantine going, Prasad?" One of my friends calls to ask.

"All good. I'm home alone, working alone. How about you?"

"Same here, buddy. I'm busy with office work, playing with the children and doing house chores whenever required." He informs me about his routine, looking all set for another day.

"So you are not going anytime soon? No hope till 3rd May," he says sympathetically.

"Yeah, I'm not surprised but a bit disappointed," I sigh.

I have been talking about the same issue – me not going home anytime soon – with many people since the last few days. It brings about a sadness that cannot be overtaken by work. Avoiding the talk may be the only way out, after all.

We have another project taking off in the company, Project 2.0, and I am a part of it. I have been trying to be a tough worker lately after sheer disappointment that my organization did not take 'work from anywhere' decision for its employees, on time, which leaves worker like me stuck alone in this situation. Without hoping that someone else talks about it, I have been pointing out this lag whenever I get the opportunity during talks.

A significant role in Project 2.0 is a relief in disguise.

I have been trying to focus on working the whole day. Good food at lunch, made by the one and only Master Chef – me – is good enough to cherish for the rest of the day.

Towards the end of the day, the news breaking everywhere is: "A large gathering of migrant workers ignored lockdown in Mumbai."

This line is smeared all around, on every news channel. Yet again, a rumour turned into a protest that the administration has complicated the situation, which the frontline warriors are finding difficult to contain. The police have taken tough actions to take control of it.

"We are not really dealing with just a pandemic, instead with insensitive humans around," I call my Baba while taking a walk on the terrace.

"Yeah, but the government should also think of them. The workers might have got frustrated and worried. Looks like the rumour has played a role in it," he continues.

"But it is just not about them. They can be just a little cautious and sensitive. There are many policemen, doctors and nurses out there, on the field, trying to take control of the situation. They are not going home to prevent any infection to their family members. This is not the way; they are protesting and it cannot be the way. And how did the police not notice these people right under their noses? I mean, areas are supposed to be sealed, so how did they reach one place all of a sudden?" I express angrily.

"Yes, you are right. We can just hope that they are not coming out and putting everyone at risk. Mumbai is already a hotspot and seeing a huge rise in cases since the past few days," he explains the situation.

"You will not be able to move out until 3rd May now. Do not worry, being in a small town, Gauri and the baby are safer there. Hope we can visit them as soon as possible. Being in the same state, we can try when there is any relaxation in the covid norms," he told me in a swift voice.

"Yeah, but be careful and travel by your own car," I sigh.

Time flies by watching epic shows like Ramayana and Mahabharata, the best of movies, TV shows and news channels along with specific office work. Lately, I have been working for limited hours. Sometimes I feel like this situation has unfolded and unearthed some of the deepest, thought-provoking actions around us. I am sure, I am not alone in feeling this way.

As of now, there are more than 2.2 million infected people. Around 0.7 million are infected in the USA alone. The total number of deceased in the world is close to 1.5 lakhs. In India, the count is standing at around 13,500 with approximately 450 deaths. Most people are still infected and there are active positive cases.

There are debates on whether a lockdown is required or not. The discussions revolve around just how effective the lockdown has been so far and how much will it help in fighting against corona. A pandemic spreads due to person-to-person contact, where even a healthy individual can be easily infected when they come in the vicinity of an infected person. A moronic statement from an inept leader of the opposition, stating that the lockdown will contain the virus and then release it once it is over, makes me laugh. In this situation, when frontline warriors are facing difficult times visiting people's houses for testing and screening, a person, without saying a word of praise, snaps baseless allegations about the government and implementation of the lockdown. Criticism is inseparable and an important part of democracy but when cynicism takes over, criticism becomes futile.

Part III: 2.0

Home Flix

"Turn your face toward the sun and the shadows fall behind you."

– Māori Proverb

For the past 2 to 3 days, I have been hearing the melodious chirping of parrots from the line of trees alongside my apartment. Although I have been trying to locate their nest in the trees around my balcony, using a pair of basic binoculars, I have not been successful yet. However, I am able to spot a sparrow's nest. Resting on the branches of a lemon tree, it is a small-sized nest with 2 white eggs. This is their home and I am ecstatic to witness this natural beauty.

Currently, all living beings on earth – except for humans – such as insects, birds and animals are roaming about freely, without any fear. Most humans are confined to their homes, while others are obligated to perform their duties to the society. Some are risking their lives for the selfless service of others. However, some people in India seem to be captive in their mindset and are creating unnecessary obstacles for the brave frontline warriors, who are providing essential services despite such hindrances. Furthermore, there are frequent news reports of political leaders disregarding the lockdown by organizing events such as birthday parties and marriage ceremonies, which reveals their lack of commitment towards the society they live in.

Making a mockery of the lockdown just for their selfish reasons or viciously harming health workers and the police is not going to help anyone. This bunch of people who are beating, spitting and urinating on health workers, partying, celebrating and arranging gatherings, spreading rumours and violating the norms set by the Indian government, are putting themselves and everyone around them in danger. People with such an ignorant mindset can worsen the situation that has already reached the 3rd stage, when the infection is spreading in the community. They ought to understand that sticking to the rules is for the well-being of their own community, neighbourhood and whole damn country.

On the other hand, India's frontline warriors are facing the virus with an iron fist. They are scared to go home because they may infect their families and others by becoming healthy carriers. In the last few days, many police constables, officers, nurses and doctors have gotten infected while doing their services.

I thought of penning down a few stories for our frontline warriors last night, based on recent events.

It is a tale of 5 people, living across different corners of India, representing those 12.5 million Covid-19 warriors. One is a 50-year-old police constable from North Delhi named Vinod. Second is Zoya from Indore, 40 years old and a doctor by profession. Third is Minal, a 30-year-old virologist from Pune. Fourth is Seema, an ASHA (Accredited Social Health Activist) worker from Bengaluru who is 45 years old. Fifth is 50-year-old Ramesh, an ambulance driver from Mumbai.

Life – 1

Since the day public gatherings were banned in New Delhi, Vinod has been posted in some or the other area to watch over the situation, along with several other constables and officers.

'Sir, what is the situation in other countries?' Vinod asks his officer while on duty.

'Not good, Vinod,' the officer replies with a sigh.

A normal day for Vinod involves patrolling around the area under his police station. Public gatherings of more than 5 are banned, in the wake of the corona situation, so they must be extra careful. Delhi is pacing up its testing and has seen only a few cases so far. Vinod visits home for lunch whenever he is nearby, whatever time in the afternoon.

'Thank god you came. Your sweet daughter is so stubborn like you, she's declined to eat anything until you are home. Let me serve you. Get her from the other room,' his wife says with a chuckle.

Vinod is married to a teacher and has 2 kids, a 14-year-old boy and a 9-year-old girl. His mother is old and stays with them. Schools and colleges have been declared closed until further notice, so his wife is at home.

After a quick meal, while spending time with kids, some messages start buzzing on the walky-talky.

'Vinod, report immediately to the police station. We must leave for someplace,' a voice says in a hurry.

'Okay, I'm coming,' he replies and leaves as soon as he possibly can.

When he arrives at the police station, he along with a few other constables and an officer, leave for Nizamuddin where there are reports of a gathering of more than 2000 people from a certain community, under one roof. They are there for a religious congregation. The news broke out and links were found when one of the visitors of this congregation died in Hyderabad and his epidemiological linkage was traced.

Those people are now being raided and asked to come out one by one. In the premise of that building, a consultation area has been set up where all these people are being checked individually. Doctors are the most vulnerable and always wear PPE (Personal Protection Equipment) kits to safeguard their lives while taking samples of a suspect's swab.

Vinod, along with the other constables, is posted outside the building to keep an eye on things and avoid any runaway cases. None of them have any PPE kits and are asked to wear clean masks while on duty. They have distributed masks to many of the poor and have also warned several people when they do not follow the lockdown norms and are roaming around unnecessarily.

'What situation these people have created,' an officer shows his resentment while standing outside with the constables.

'Sir, any clue as to why they were here?' Vinod asks.

'No, not yet. What could the grave situation be that they had to assemble or be under the same roof in such a large number, even after a lockdown had been declared?'

'What will happen now? Why are we not arresting them?'

'Not sure, let us wait and see. Anyways, we cannot arrest them until they are all checked by the doctors.'

There are buses arriving and people are being boarded into them. Journalists are reporting the news from quite a distance but the police must be present at all times to keep a watch.

'Why the hell could these people not gather before the lockdown or just after and save their asses as well as those of the others?' one constable mutters.

'Yeah, I am also wondering the same. What were they doing all these days? They look so normal as if we are taking them on a pilgrimage,' Vinod says while watching them from the gate.

'Just keep a close eye on these people; they should not spit outside or talk among themselves in groups. Better yet, ask them to close the windows and allow only one person to sit on each seat.' An officer comes from inside after meeting the doctors and asks them to rush.

'What happened, sir?' Vinod asks after a few shouts at the people boarding.

'There are people with severe symptoms among them. The doctors are still taking samples and checking the others.'

'Ohh, okay. So, what is next for us?'

'Guys, I was discussing with the doctors and we need to take extra precautions.'

'Like what, sir?'

'I mean, it is better if we do not go home as we are completely exposed to these patients with severe symptoms. I, myself, will not be going. Okay, do one thing once we are out of here. Go home, get your clothes and some basic things to the station. I will make arrangements for you all to stay there. If possible, do not go inside yourself and pick up the stuff; keep a safe distance from the family members at home. You understood?'

'Yes sir,' all the constables say in one voice. Thoughts flick their minds while all this is going on. Thoughts flock to their minds and they realise they are not alone when standing quietly on duty after hearing those tough words from an officer.

Later that evening, they found that the person who headed the gathering was missing and was not with these people. Out of more than 2300 people, 200 were found to be positive for the coronavirus and the rest had been quarantined. The initial reports said that in the 1st week of March, there were more than 8,000 people who came to that place and attended this religious congregation.

Vinod, along with the other constables, collected his belongings from home, ensuring all precautions were taken, and arrived at the police station.

'See, I understand the inconvenience, but it is not right for us to take this freaking invisible thing we get exposed to outside daily into our homes. Our families will be vulnerable, especially the kids and elders. Believe me, there are many like us in the force who are posted in hotspots and are not visiting their homes to safeguard their families in other cities and states,' the officer calmly tells them all.

'I have taken permission from the top and arranged these rooms at the station for all of us. We must stay here till the situation comes under control. We all are duty-bound and public safety is our priority. All understood?'

'Yes sir,' all say in one voice, one spirit, one commitment.

Over the next few days, finding epidemiological links of those at the congregation led to around 23,000 in quarantine and a surge in positive cases on an everyday basis. The number of cases is already expected to grow with an increase in tests across India. They led the way and today around

30% of the positive cases belong to these people. They never helped in something good for the country but made the life of our warriors even more difficult by their moronic and sinister activities. It does not matter which community, caste or religion one belongs to, no one has the authority to harm others and make life difficult for them. It is not sane to do so. Humanity is to do and be good to others.

With a commitment to keeping people safe by asking them to stay indoors, many of these warriors are doing their duties across India. They spend long hours on duty outside their homes in order to keep people, who can stay home themselves, safe. Some irritants are making it difficult for these people to visit their homes anytime soon.

They are warriors with just one mask on their faces. They are the warriors who are fighting on the battlefield with no PPE kits.

Life – 2

Zoya, 40 years old, is living a simple life in Indore. She has been practising in a government hospital in the city for the last 10 years. Every day, like a perfect housewife, she takes care of her family, starting from cooking in the morning to taking her kid's homework in the evening. Being a daughter herself, she takes care of her own parents as well as her in-laws. Even after handling all these responsibilities at home, she is always kind to her patients. And why not? It has been her dream to become a doctor, and her father left no stone unturned to support her.

Back in January, when the coronavirus cases were on the rise in China and had started appearing in other parts of the world too, it became apparent that the doctor community was going to have a tough time ahead to fight this invisible evil. Every day since then, doctors and researchers have been trying to figure out every possible way to find a cure or a vaccine to save lives.

'What is this infection doing to people around the world?' her husband asks during his morning tea after watching the recent news feeds.

'This is a virus for which we do not have a vaccine or cure anywhere in the world. It spreads from person to person – or what we call P2P – in one of its stages. Once a person is infected, the symptoms are seen from day 2 to day 14. Also, this virus can survive on surfaces for a few hours. Infections have spread from China, as per the data till now, and the reason behind this is still speculative,' she explains the details to him.

'What are the symptoms?'

'Well, it shows very common symptoms in the body like fever, cold, cough, body ache and numbness. The evil thing is that many of these symptoms may come one at a time or all at once.'

Indore was a Clean City Award winner for the 3rd time in a row in 2019. It has been a journey for this city; from being a heritage place to the financial capital of Madhya Pradesh to the cleanest city in India. Indore finds its roots in the 16th century, and later in the 18th century, when the Maratha Empire was ruling this region.

Today, this clean city is facing the pandemic with an iron fist. People's travel histories are being traced, tests are being conducted, people are kept in quarantine and the lockdown has been strictly imposed after seeing a surge in infectious people every day.

'I have to go to Ranipura today to take some samples,' she informs her husband.

'Okay. Are those patients linked to the Delhi case?'

'Not sure as of now.'

'Be careful.'

Zoya reaches the hospital and starts getting ready for her visit. She is accompanied by another lady doctor and a couple of ASHA health workers.

'Let's get ready. Put on your PPE kit,' she tells her companion.

It takes time to don and doff the PPE. It covers her from head to toe – the clothes, skin, nose, ears as well as the mouth – providing protection from viral and bacterial infections. Doctors and nurses cannot maintain social distancing while seeing patients. They must be close to them for prolonged periods. It can involve taking down the patient's history and symptoms as well as conducting physical and routine check-ups when found positively infectious and admitted.

The team reaches the location while moving through the small lanes of that area.

An unfortunate incident takes place and the doctors must return without taking any samples of patients with symptoms.

After coming back to the hospital, she narrates the horror they witnessed in broad daylight.

'We were going to a patient's home that was situated in a small lane. Suddenly, people started coming out of their homes and a few, who were already on the roads, started moving rapidly towards the doctors and workers. In no time, a mob was hurling stones and running after us with bamboo poles or whatever they could find. They were abusing, shouting, hurling stones and running after us.

I have never seen scenes like that. It was frightening. We somehow fled from the mob. I am injured but not scared at all. We cannot get scared when performing our duties.'

Do these sick and cowardly people hear the brave doctors? They are putting their lives at risk while serving people during this health emergency. Their selfless commitments towards their duties are being abused. A doctor is said to be the face of God, either one dies in his hands or survives a critical illness. They also have families that are vulnerable due to their consistent closeness to patients.

They bring the much-needed hope that every human being requires in this situation. They are fighting this micrometre-long virus closely. We are humans, not animals who cannot differentiate between the good and bad in others and ourselves. No one should be allowed to abuse doctors in any situation and confronting them during a health emergency in the country is a sinful act.

Life – 3

"She needed a hero so that is what she became."

– Proverb

In these difficult times of the pandemic, many of our frontline warriors are women. Apart from doctors, nurses, police officers, constables and health and social workers, there are other heroes as well who are researching and working on faster testing kits and vaccine development.

Minal is a virologist and lives in Pune. She heads a team of 10 to 11 members, who are all working on developing indigenous test kits. Since the coronavirus outbreak in India, they have started working on it expeditiously. They are already running out of time and taking the normal 3 to 4 months cannot be acceptable or useful.

'It was done in record time – 6 weeks instead of 3 or 4 months,' Minal says, describing her team's journey in making these kits available.

'It was an emergency, so I took this on as a challenge. I must serve my nation, after all.

Our kit gives the diagnosis in 2.5 hours while the imported testing kits take 6 to 7 hours,' she adds, giving further information to the media and everyone she interacts with.

She was pregnant while working on developing these test kits, but still led her team to success. The next day, when the kits were submitted for evaluation, she delivered a baby girl. Her daughter will be so proud of her mother once she gets to know that she has been so strong and determined to serve the nation while taking good care of her in the womb.

Life – 4

It is the story of one ASHA healthcare worker from Bengaluru. Seema, 45 years old, lives in a ward in North Bengaluru. She has a small happy family of 4, including 2 kids and a husband, who works in the Bengaluru Municipal Corporation.

Seema is one among a million workers in India who work for the society. She serves the nation by motivating women to give birth in hospitals, bringing children to immunization clinics, encouraging family planning, treating basic illnesses and injuries with first aid, keeping demographic records and improving village/ward sanitation. An ASHA worker like her connects people to various healthcare systems and helps them access these systems with ease. They have a tough job to do when they see a few people in the Indian villages still lagging in sanitisation. Many are unaware of the availability of basic healthcare systems provided by the Government of India from time to time. These may include new schemes introduced by the government, like providing insurance cover for 40% of the poor and vulnerable population or building toilets, and may include arranging free health camps that offer basic vaccines for their infants. They take care of each activity with the same enthusiasm, connecting the local population with health care. Despite so much effort, they are paid less, such that they can barely manage their homes and it becomes necessary for their spouses to work.

Since the coronavirus outbreak has been seen in India, they have been occupied with activities like carrying out surveillance following a reported case, helping doctors figure those cases out and tracing homes in their area. At times, they even help local authorities in sanitising the area after multiple cases are reported, to prevent further spread of the infection. The lockdown has made their routes accessible by easing out the traffic but the job is still tough and has become even tougher in this situation.

This is a usual day of surveillance work and she is accompanied by another lady worker along with a doctor. They are in an area where a positive Covid-19 case was found yesterday. They must now find the patient's connections – whom he met in the last few days. They also need to enable the doctor to take samples in order to proceed with the medication in case the connections are found to have multiple symptoms and get them hospitalised, if needed.

The work is quite straightforward and methodical in approach but risky as the chances of getting infected are large if precautions are not strictly adhered to. In such surveillance, the doctor or nurse, donned with PPE kits, will take the samples and do the necessary work that requires close interaction with the suspect or patient. ASHA workers mostly have one mask, an apron and gloves.

'How are your kids, Seema?' the doctor asks in a gushing manner.

'They are good and happy, madam. Their father has not been going to work for a few days now so they are enjoying time with him, playing all the time. What else they can want? No school no homework,' she replies lovingly like she can talk for hours about her children.

'Yes, very nice to hear that. Let them play. They should be engaged at home as much as possible and should not think of going out,' the doctor instructs compassionately. While saying this, she looks at her brave subordinates.

Suddenly, they see a mob of 50 to 60 people coming towards them; they are already horrified by the reports of attacks on people like them by mobs across India.

'Do not worry or tremble, try to stay strong. I am with you, okay?' the doctor tries to keep their spirits up.

In a few minutes, the mob gets nearer and a few people from the mob step out to come closer.

'Why are you here?' a man asks in a rude tone.

'We are here to take samples of people who met a patient and have symptoms,' the doctor replies strongly, in an unmoved spirit, after seeing the mob.

'Do not speak any more, just get the hell out of this area. We did not call you, we do not want you here, we do not need your help,' the man raises his voice and the mob shouts in one voice, asking them to go away.

They helplessly leave, running away from the place of incident in a hurry.

'A huge crowd of minority community members manhandled us and told us that we should not inquire about anyone's Covid-19 symptoms. They even shouted that they could die of Covid-19 and we should not be worried. They even snatched documents pertaining to the surveillance work, our mobile phones and other valuables,' Seema explains to the police while reporting the horrific incident.

'Sir, how come they can ask us to go away? Are they not afraid of the pandemic or what? We are helping them by being on the field, by locating the person with the symptoms,' she asks virtuously.

After listening to her calmly, the police official was deeply moved and tried to console her. He assured her that they could ask for police support whenever they wanted for such surveillance.

Healthcare workers like Seema are frontline warriors who have already put their families at risk and are vulnerable to infections when they are on duty. A few people seem to be making it more difficult for themselves and the people around them, putting their lives at risk.

Life – 5

Amid the Covid-19 pandemic, the role of ambulance drivers has become more crucial than ever before. One such ambulance driver is Ramesh, who has been working tirelessly since the beginning of the lockdown to ensure that patients get timely medical assistance.

Ramesh's day starts early in the morning by sanitising the ambulance. He then puts on his Personal Protective Equipment (PPE) and begins his shift. His ambulance is equipped with an oxygen cylinder and other necessary equipment to provide basic medical care during transportation.

Due to the lockdown, Ramesh faces several challenges while transporting patients. He often encounters barricades and police checkpoints on the roads, which delay his arrival at the hospital. However, he remains calm and patient, knowing that his job is vital in saving lives.

One of Ramesh's most memorable experiences during the lockdown was when he transported a critically ill Covid-19 patient to the hospital. The patient's oxygen levels were dangerously low and he needed immediate medical attention. Ramesh drove the ambulance at high speed, making sure he followed all safety protocols.

Despite the challenges, Ramesh reached the hospital in time and the patient received prompt medical care. The patient's family later called Ramesh to thank him for his prompt service and for saving their loved one's life.

Ramesh is just one of the many unsung heroes who are risking their lives every day to help others during these challenging times. Their selfless service and dedication to their job are truly commendable and inspiring.

Part IV: 3.0

A Star in the Sky

Day 38

1st May 2020

Well, it is the 38th day of the lockdown in India and we all now have a different routine in life. Staying at home and working may have been everyone's dream at some point in their careers and a few are seeing it fulfilled in this way. The market is closed, except for essentials. Passenger transport is also shut down. Since the independence era, there has never been a time when the Indian Railways have been shut; it has been 38 straight days now that no passenger trains have run on the tracks except the cargo trains that carry essential goods.

'India will remain in lockdown for another 2 weeks after the 2nd phase ends on 3rd May,' the media reports.

"So, it is official then," I tell myself after seeing the news everywhere on TV channels and news feeds.

This sort of news hurts less now as I have become accustomed to my routine and am already prepared for an extension. It was apparent after seeing the surge in cases across many states in India.

At this moment, the active Covid-19 cases stand at around 45,000 with nearly 1 million tests being conducted across the country. The deceased count stands at 1200-odd, while about 10,000 have already recovered. The total number of cases in the world is topping at 3.5 million, whereas in the USA alone stands at 1 million cases – the highest so far. Certainly, tests cannot suddenly be conducted at large in a country like India but a sense of opportunity to increase them in the coming days is necessary. This can be done by arranging PPEs and various testing kits faster and in enough quantity in order to do extensive testing and provide quicker results. India has converted this challenge of manufacturing masks, PPEs and indigenous test kits into an opportunity and quickly shifted the gears of the medical industry, reducing the country's economic burden of procuring or importing them from other countries. This will make us self-reliant in this situation, which doesn't look like it's getting over anytime soon.

Indians may find it difficult to continue practising social distancing as we are quite social. We like meeting each other and taking care of each other – our neighbours, relatives and friends. Even if this culture might see a slow death in some parts of metro cities, it is our prevailing behaviour. We may not be meeting everyone in person but keeping in touch through the telephone or video calls is common. Social and physical distancing cannot keep you away from your loved ones for too long – we will find surely a way to get rid of the situation.

Day 41

4th May 2020

Tomorrow, on 5th May, my son will complete one month in this world. He has gained some weight now and his eyes have been wide open for a few days. We've decided to name him 'Megh', which we chose from a lot of names that we liked and heard from several people. Megh seems to be a calm and active kid. I have heard that he does not cry unless he feels uncomfortable and needs a diaper change. He seems to be communicating in his own way by making crying noises whenever he needs to be cleaned. Once he is clean and comfortable, he is ready to play and eagerly looks around him with his big, brown eyes, tracking his mother's every movement. It is impressive how he already has a strong sense of sight at such a young age. As of now, I have not been fortunate enough to see him in person and have only seen him on video calls since his birth, which is my only option at the moment. Although I am looking for every possible way to get home, it does not seem to be anytime soon or before lockdown 3.0 ends, which is 17th May. On a personal level, it may feel more overwhelming but when it comes to safeguarding the health ecosystem of the country, it feels no less than being a soldier. There are soldiers at borders who sacrifice their family time for the nation's safety; staying at home until the authorities instruct and following all necessary precautions is the least one can do at this time.

Yeah, another lockdown of 2 weeks is starting today, though there are some relaxed norms seen across many states. Every district in every state is divided into green, orange and red zones, and these districts will have different restrictions. Industries are set to open with limited workforce in the green zones. Activities in the markets will start and small shops will open from today in all 3 zones so that people have access to essential services. Malls, barber shops and restaurants will remain closed in all zones. Containment zones will remain shut and face curfew.

Public transport will remain off the road. Interstate movement will be allowed only during an emergency or for essential services. Though passes have been issued by state administrations for migrant students who are stranded and people in an emergency, the decision to allow passage through the state remains with local state governments and administrations. Very few trains are running on the tracks, that too for migrant labourers only.

State governments are worried about their dipping revenues due to the shutdown as markets are down and tax collections are at a historical low. Ministers and top bureaucrats are laying out strategies and plans to bring normalcy to the states. To get rid of the economic losses, the first step taken is the opening of liquor shops across many states. There are also a few states where the sale of liquor is already banned but other states have given a nod to the sale of liquor in stand-alone shops with restrictions on the limit. Limitations set by most of the governments come as a joke and are not favourable to curbing Covid-19 and following guidelines.

From the next day itself, people are standing in long queues even before the shops open and there is chaos all around. Very long queues, clashes while getting in line to purchase, forgetting guidelines of social distancing and people carelessly coming out, risking their and their families' lives. This is the scene in most parts of the country. In the process of minimising our economic losses, we could not wait for another 2 weeks or some more time to see a dip in everyday cases. If the situation worsens, who will be responsible and will we be in a position to take control again?

6th May 2020

Suddenly, at around 8 PM, I get a call from Ashish's wife.

"Papa (Ashish's father) is no more. Since Ashish is alone, can you please accompany him?" she pleads.

"Oh......, yeah."

I am taken aback upon hearing the shocking news but try to remain composed. My mind begins to race through the various images and memories of my interactions with him during his visit to Bengaluru. My throat feels constricted and it is difficult to swallow as I struggle to process the news. Ashish, like me, is also stranded in a different location away from his family, which only adds to the gravity of the situation. Losing someone dear, especially one's parent, is a monumental loss that cannot be substituted or compensated for.

I quickly grab the keys, lock the door and leave.

"We need to figure out a way to travel as soon as possible," he says with a sense of urgency in his voice. "We can start by contacting the local authorities and see if any special arrangements are being made for people who need to travel urgently."

As he spoke, I could see deep sorrow in his eyes and concern to find a solution. I take a deep breath and try to compose myself. I know that I need to be strong for him as he is going through a difficult time.

"Okay, let's do that," I reply, nodding my head in agreement. "We'll find a way to get there, no matter what."

And with that, we begin our search for a way to travel to Mumbai, hoping and praying that he is able to reach in time to bid farewell to his father.

For the next few minutes, we check our phones and glance through every official communication and notification for ways to travel to another state.

"Why don't we ask our landlord for help? He would surely have some genuine contacts," Ashish suggests.

We quickly go to our landlord's home, which is just behind our apartment, and inform him about our urgency to travel back to Mumbai.

Our landlord immediately makes phone calls to a few people. One person, who has a travel agency, agrees to drive him to Mumbai. We are all aware that there may be obstacles during the journey, particularly at the border areas where authorities question everyone. They even quarantine anyone who displays any symptoms and refuse entry into the state if it is not for emergency services, but he must travel.

"The driver will arrive in 2 hours," the landlord confirms, "but we need to apply for a pass immediately as it is already past 10 PM."

After checking all possible online options to apply for a pass and not finding any, we decide to go to the nearest police station, where the local authorities could help.

I drive him to the police station after grabbing as much as cash we can manage. We go inside and check with the person available. We get help and a pass in our hands without any authority's signature. Authority signatures are given during official hours and for some extended time but not this late. Leaving without it is also a sort of risk since Ashish needs to cross the state border.

"This would help I am sure," I say in an assured voice.

After waiting for some more time at the police station, the car arrives and Ashish gets into it after giving me a swift hug. It will take him about 17 hours to reach home, not to mention an enormous amount of time that could be spent in making the cross-border authorities understand the situation and explain his urgency to travel, if stopped at a check post.

His dad suffered a heart attack while taking a walk close to home. He is the only son and has 2 sisters. His journey to Mumbai is going to be a long and emotional one as he reflects on the memories he shared with his father. The loss is truly unimaginable.

I drive back home in complete numbness, devoid of any thoughts.

Mid-May 2020

My company has been sanitising and cleaning the office premises and workstations promptly. They have asked if anyone is handling any critical work, in which case they can arrange for a few employees to go to the office on a weekly basis. They want to limit the number of employees working from the office for safety reasons. They have asked other employees to continue working from home and this has been enabled till 18th May. The dates keep extending. Other major corporates prefer to work from home till mid-June and have given up-front notices to their employees, as I come to know from friends. Certainly, one doubts if offices can start anytime soon. As per the human resource department, these decisions are being discussed with utmost alertness in the wake of the situation around them. I hope they make proactive decisions for their hard-working employees. Many companies have already given work from home (anywhere) after seeing the situation in Feb/March month. In general, an employee will have an increased level of confidence in the company if decisions are taken on time.

In the last few days, I have been trying to get information about passes and migrants from one state to another. How is a state treating people who are entering in their own vehicles with passes? Some states are screening and asking them to stay quarantined in their homes if they are asymptomatic or advising institutional quarantine if they have severe symptoms.

"Sir, when can we leave for Nagpur?" I call and ask Sanjeev Sir, with whom I have been planning to travel to my hometown in a personal vehicle.

"We can leave on 18th May if the situation gets better and we see that the administration is not putting us in institutional quarantine. Have you got any information on this?" he asks.

"People are moving around with passes, this is what I have got to know. In my hometown, people who have arrived from outside need to visit the government hospital to get checked."

I explained that home quarantine would be suggested if asymptomatic.

"Also, one of my friends from back home told me that we should apply in the state we are travelling and get checked for sure," I continue.

"There are chances that our neighbours might complain about our homecoming to the administration, so it's better to get checked upfront so that we can show them the clean reports," I chuckle while trying to make a point.

"Okay, yeah. Even in Prayagraj – my hometown – one of our tenants came back from another city and someone called the local police. They came home and asked the tenant to go back or be in institutional quarantine. It didn't matter if he was symptomatic or not. Things are really happening this way and there should be no hard feelings."

"Oh really," I reciprocate.

Yeah, no hard feelings. Neighbourhood is one social term that covers a broader meaning, where people around help, share, care, laugh, brawl, party, play, pray and do many more activities together at one point or another. But now, if they are complaining, even when they like or dislike their neighbours, it is another kind of awareness. This will protect their neighbourhood from becoming vulnerable. Also, if one is travelling to some other place, getting himself checked in a hospital on reaching the destination will ensure not only the safety of his own family but that of the entire neighbourhood.

After all, when we travel by road, we must cross 5 major states, including the source and destination states. So, our plan to go back to our hometown is now completely dependent on the lifting of the lockdown after its 3rd phase, the relaxations given and the Covid-19 situation across India. It also depends on his college's management, which has decided on a pay cut in case people are leaving the city and returning after a fortnight and may not be able to join immediately due to travel restrictions.

There is uncertainty all around, be it unlocking the market, lifting the travel ban, travelling to hometowns, getting permission to work from our hometowns or keeping the situation in control. Nothing is visible through the gloomy weather around us. Another uncertainty comes in the guidelines given by different states across India, following the basic rules imposed by the central government. They are continuously revising and publishing these rules and we must keep a follow-up on such notifications if we want to travel.

Part V: 4.0

Homecoming

"The darkness that follows a sunset is never so dark that it can change the inevitability of a sunrise."

– Unknown

Day 61

24th May 2020

Today we complete 2 months of lockdown at a stretch. I still remember the day when the Prime Minister announced the lockdown one evening. India has moved from a few hundred cases to 1,30,000 as of now. There have been hurdles in implementing the lockdown properly and its success or failure cannot be understood with just the number of cases India has seen while being in lockdown. We still have a long way to go as this situation will continue; it does not seem to be stopping anytime soon.

This viral disease spreads by coming in contact with an infected person. Finding traces of the patient and putting them in quarantine is a herculean task when it comes to social attachment and the awareness level of all 'One Thirty-Five Crore' Indians.

The Next Morning

"After a gap of 2 months, domestic passenger flight operations will resume from Monday, 25th May, amid reluctance by various states to open up their airports in view of the rising cases of the novel coronavirus," the media reports.

This news will give hope to many lives who could not visit and help their families stay safe. Many have been stuck in different cities and were taken aback when the lockdown was imposed. Hardly a week back, the Indian Railways started running special trains from the national capital to 15 states. This too raised the hopes of thousands of stranded workers who are trying to reach home amid the national lockdown, which has taken away their work and their much-needed income – their daily wages.

I was probably waiting for this news so that I could visit my family. Despite planning to travel by road for a long time, I knew it was not going to be easy to cover 1000 miles without taking breaks and crossing 4 state borders, which are open for essential services alone.

"It might not be safe to travel right now. I will plan after 10 to 15 days to avoid any panic travel," I inform my family.

Now there are a few relaxations given by the local authorities in Bengaluru, and after quite a long time, I will be taking my bike out to drive to my cousin's place, of course with all due precautions. She shifted to Bengaluru from Jabalpur due to her husband's official transfer. A much-needed change after more than 2 months; stepping away from the friendliest place during these isolated times.

Day 79

Finally, the time has come.

"I have booked a flight to Nagpur on 17th June. We will then visit Gauri and my newborn baby," I tell my father on the call. Nagpur is the nearest airport to my hometown.

I am delighted with the thought of going home and seeing my parents, my wife and son but at the same time, scared that I might travel with a symptomatic or asymptomatic co-passenger and get infected. I'm not afraid for myself but for parents who are aged, as well as for my wife and son who are still vulnerable to infections.

Nevertheless, I am ready and acquiring every possible information on how to get tested at the nearest hospital in my hometown and stay in quarantine for the required number of days, once I reach there.

Suddenly...

"Your flight booking is cancelled due to unavoidable circumstances."

I receive this message just a couple of days before my flight.

This sudden cancellation of the flight, without warning, has shattered all my hopes and excitement. I am aware that transportation by air has been resumed with conditions, but experiencing the cancellation has made the situation feel even more frustrating.

While exploring other options, I decide to book a ticket to Indore, which is close to my wife's hometown. I am now waiting anxiously, with my fingers crossed, hoping that this flight will not be cancelled. I have also informed my parents and wife of the change of plans and let them know that I have now booked a flight to Indore. I will be coming home along with both, my wife and son. Despite the unforeseen challenges, I am trying to remain optimistic and hopeful that everything will work out in the end.

16th June 2020: Travel Day

Since there are relaxations in transportation, cabs are now allowed to take passengers to the airport or railway stations. I reach the airport at night; my flight is early the next morning at 5.45 AM.

It is an uncommon scene at one of India's busiest airports. This airport, which typically accommodates 20 million passengers annually and is known for its bustling activity, particularly at night when there is a lot of air traffic to and from destinations outside of India, now sees only a few hundred passengers stranded in one location for an extended period, waiting for their flights.

In this time of heightened panic and caution, it is evident that everyone at the airport is taking precautions to protect themselves and others. Nearly everyone is seen wearing at least one mask, if not two, and are seated as if wary of anyone nearby who might infect them. Thoughts of the current situation are at the forefront of people's minds.

The airport staff stands out in their efforts to maintain a clean and safe environment. They can be seen frequently sanitizing all the trolleys and the surrounding premises, working hard to ensure that the airport remains as clean and safe as possible. Seeing this level of dedication and commitment to public health and safety is heartening, and it underscores the importance of taking personal responsibility in times of crisis.

I remain seated at the airport and even doze off for a while, taking extra precautions to ensure my safety. I am covered with a jacket and cap and am also wearing 2 masks to protect myself from any potential risk of getting infected by the virus. I am also carrying just one small bag as I want to avoid any baggage that might need to be checked in and handled by others.

I know that these precautions might seem excessive to some, but I feel it is important to take every possible measure to protect myself and others from the risks associated with air travel. By being mindful of what I bring with me and how I cover myself, I hope to minimise the likelihood of any potential exposure to the infection while at the airport or during travel.

I get into the plane on time and reach Indore by 7:45 AM. There are few ambulances waiting at the airport. After enquiring about them, I get to know that the authorities had found a few infected persons who had landed in Indore on a flight from Dubai. They are being asked to get admitted into a hospital and isolate themselves, while others are advised to quarantine. My wife's hometown is another 150 km from here and my brother-in-law has sent his car to pick me up so that public transport can be avoided.

The wait is finally over...

After a 3-hour journey by road, I finally arrive and reunite with my wife and son. As soon as I see my little one, I can barely contain my excitement and immediately want to hold him in my arms. Despite having seen him on video calls, seeing him in person – his eyes wide-open, rosy cheeks and tiny hands – is an incredible feeling, not to mention an emotional one.

After exchanging a few words from a safe distance, I quickly bathe and sanitise myself. I have decided to go into self-quarantine for at least 7 days and avoid holding my son during this time, which I now realise will be a real challenge. Nonetheless, I am committed to taking all necessary precautions to keep myself and my family safe.

Even after the 5th day, I do not show any symptoms and it seems fine as time passes.

Now that I am reunited with Gauri and our son, Megh, my thoughts turn to my parents, who have been alone and isolated during these tough 3 months. I can only imagine how difficult it must have been for them to manage their daily needs in a small town that was closed for 3 months and has even now only partly opened up.

"Would you be okay with leaving tomorrow to visit my parents?" I ask Gauri. "It has been 6 days and I don't appear to be infected. We can take our own car to minimise the risk."

"Of course, let's go as Aai and Baba also might be waiting for us," Gauri replies positively. "We will take all the necessary precautions and avoid interaction with strangers during the journey."

The next day, we leave Gauri's home and I inform my parents that we are on our way to them.

24th June 2020

"Having empathy is the biggest virtue of being a human."

– Unknown

When I was in Bengaluru and the lockdown was suddenly imposed, my life came to a halt and it felt like it would be a long time till this moment arrived. However, during this difficult time, something remarkable happened.

People stepped forward to support their neighbours and even strangers in need. Some professions turned into "Frontline Workers and then Real Warriors" as they dedicated themselves to serving, caring, feeding and supporting millions of people selflessly and tirelessly. Despite the personal challenges when people lost loved ones, they fought for strangers at the same time. The future seems uncertain at this very moment, but these actions will continue to inspire millions to do their part in the upcoming challenging times. The decision of keeping the nation in lockdown for 2 months might seem questionable but it is subjective and up to one's own opinion. No matter whether the decision made was good or bad, looking at the number of cases across other countries in the world and India, it seems to be in our favour as of now; however, it may take a few years before we can make any judgements, if we must.

India has a strong tradition of close family relationships and emotions are deeply engraved in our DNA.

My parents are eagerly awaiting our arrival, and have made all the necessary preparations that might be required once we reach home. They have been looking forward to meeting their grandchild for a long time; the challenging circumstances made it difficult for them to travel.

We have taken a road trip on this route a few times before and I can confidently say that the traffic is 70% less than usual. My hometown – Betul. We arrive after 8 hours of travel, including a couple of breaks at the safest possible places. This is the shortest time taken of all, as the roads were mostly empty and there was not much traffic. My mother holds a small traditional ceremony when we enter the house with a burst of joy. They have embarked on a new journey as grandparents with broad smiles on their faces and a twinkle in their eyes.

After all, my father has found his favourite 'Guddu' (a commonly used nickname in Indian households) in 'Megh'.

www.ingramcontent.com/pod-product-compliance
Lightning Source LLC
La Vergne TN
LVHW041114150826
845673LV00007B/2052

* 9 7 9 8 8 9 1 3 3 3 8 4 0 *